D1436417

Wilberforce the Whale

Wilberforce
the
Whale

Leslie Coleman

Illustrated by John Laing

BLACKIE: GLASGOW and LONDON

ISBN 0 216 89621 5

Blackie and Son Limited
Bishopbriggs, Glasgow G64 2NZ
5 Fitzhardinge Street, London 1H 0DL

Filmset by Thomson Litho, East Kilbride, Scotland
Printed in Great Britain by Robert MacLehose & Co. Ltd., Glasgow

Wilberforce
would like to say
a special hallo to
Ben, Julie-Anne, Stephen and Max.

Contents

I

Wilberforce Gets a Letter

Melody, the shrimp, was tidying her cave. She had swept the sandy floor quite smooth and clean so that it was ready for her to snuggle into comfortably if she felt like a nap, and she had seen to the larder, a curtain of red and green seaweed which hung all across one wall. She was just straightening the pebbles which decorated a ledge at the back of her little home, when the sun, which had been shining down through the sea right into the cave's mouth, was suddenly blotted out.

Melody pirouetted round—fiss-ss-z!—and saw that, where a minute before the sun had been dappling the sandy sea-bed with gold and silver stripes, there was now a great mountain wall, blue-black at the top, and shading off to cream-green underneath, where it met the sand.

'It's Wilberforce,' she whispered to herself, and her feathery feelers quivered with delight. In an instant she had darted out of her home—per-shoo-oot!—and was racing down beside the towering body beyond. Pfut-pfut-pfut-pfut-pfut!—she swam as fast as she could, but it was some seconds and nearly twenty yards of distance before she came level with an eye, and some three feet below it the beginning of a huge mouth curled in an amiable smile.

'Hallo, Wilberforce,' called Melody.

'And hallo to you, my little friend, my mopsy-mate, my pal, my little shrimpy comrade,' replied the whale; for that is what the blue-black mountain really was. 'And the top of the warm, sea-green and watery morning to you.'

'You're a bit late,' said Melody, standing on her tail like a seahorse. 'What kept you?'

'Luncheon,' said Wilberforce, 'the mid-morning snack, the er little bite-to-keep-body-and-soul-together—delicious, delectable and titillating to the palate! The cuttlefish this morning down in the valley where the bladder-wrack grows were more than usually succulent. I had a third helping . . . I really *must* put myself on a diet . . . my figure, you know!'

Melody chanted:

> 'Wilberforce, the whale,
> Has a very long tail,
> And his mouth is as big
> As a ninety gallon pail.'

'True!' grinned the good-natured whale;

'the mouth is large, but it has to supply a large interior.'

Melody continued:

'He doesn't leave a crumb,
And Wilberforce's tum
Is as tight after dinner
As a drum, drum, drum!'

'If you were not my personal, permanent, perennial shrimp-friend,' grinned Wilberforce, 'I should catch you a spank with my flipper-fin. As it is I shall withdraw with dignity up above and take in a breath of fresh air.' And the mighty whale floated lazily up through the water towards the surface—blubble-ubble-obble-obble-ibble-ebble-abble-abble-sfisch! For whales, as you know, breath air like animals through a blow-hole in their forehead, and not through gills like a fish.

'Don't be long!' called Melody, the shrimp. 'You promised to play this afternoon, you know.'

'All in good time,' replied Wilberforce, and the top of his body disappeared through the mirror-surface of the water, leaving only his white tum visible like the bottom of a large ocean liner.

So Melody started to make miniature sand-storms from the sea-bed with her tail to pass the time. She had just raised a large and particularly successful storm, when round the corner of a rock covered in red leaf-weed scuttled a crab. His eight weaving legs pushed him busily sideways while in his claws he held a square of white sailcloth at least six times as big as himself. Puffing with concentrated determination he dragged his load importantly towards the shrimp, and he was so deep in the job, that if Melody hadn't given a quick flip with her tail to shoot her clear of the sea-bed there would have been a collision—wish-per-soof!

'Hey, look where you're going, Nelson!' she cried.

'Oh, it's you, Melody, is it?' said Nelson, the crab. 'Sorry I didn't see you; it's an awkward thing to carry, this . . .' and he waved his largest unoccupied clipper in the direction of the white cloth.

'I should think it must be,' said Melody. 'What's it for?'

'It's a letter,' said Nelson; 'I'm working for the Post Office during the school holidays, and it's for Wilberforce. Have you seen him?'

'He's up breathing,' said Melody. 'If it's a letter specially for him, I think I'd better let him know,' and she made a series of rapid swishes up through the water—sfish-sfish-sfish-sfish-sfish—and started to hammer with her tiny feet on the whale's great side.

Wilberforce put his head below the surface. 'Huh-huh-huh! Stop tickling me,' he giggled. 'You'll make me choke.'

'But there's a letter,' said Melody.

'A letter?'

'Yes, it's addressed to you.'

'To me?'

'Yes! Nelson's brought it specially. He's working for the Post Office during the school holidays.'

'A letter for me! Oh, then I'd better come down,' said Wilberforce, and he swam down in a rather important way as is natural with someone who has had a personal letter personally addressed to him.

'Good afternoon, Nelson,' said Wilberforce. 'One tells me that one has a letter for one!'

'That's right; it's over there,' said Nelson pointing to the piece of folded sailcloth.

'Thank you very much for your trouble in bringing it, my cetaceous, and generally my crab-like, little Post Office official.'

'Not at all,' replied Nelson; 'it's all part of the service. What do you think's in it?'

'Well, now,' said Wilberforce, 'let me see!' And he flipped his body up through the water with his great fluke-tail on top, and his nose and right eye down on the sand looking straight at the letter. 'It isn't a bill,' said Wilberforce, 'because it hasn't got one of those oval transparent windows in it,' and he flipped his tail so that his left eye surveyed the white square. 'And it isn't a receipt,' he said, 'because I have never had any bills to pay in my life. And I don't think,' he said, twisting round again so that both eyes now looked down on it with a slight squint, 'I don't think it's an invitation to have tea with the Queen at Buckingham Palace, because it isn't addressed to Sir Wilberforce Whale Esquire.'

'Oh, open it, open it!' begged Nelson and Melody together. 'Then we shall *know*.'

'It's a bit difficult to undo,' said Wilberforce. 'My fins are rather big . . . perhaps, Nelson, you . . .'

But before he could finish the sentence, Nelson had unfolded the sailcloth and smoothed it out on a convenient rock to show the writing. Wilberforce glared at the letters in a very concentrated way.

'There's a "D",' he said.

'Go on,' said Melody.

'Don't hurry me,' grumbled Wilberforce. 'I like to take my time, be deliberate, leisurely . . .'

'You mean you're slow,' said Nelson.

'Well, it's all right,' complained the whale, 'when it's printed like books, but this hand-

written stuff needs experience, expertise, er enterprise, er . . .'

'Oh, come on, let Nelson do it,' cried Melody. 'He's in the Post Office, he can read anything.'

'Oh, all right,' said Wilberforce. 'What does it say?'

So Nelson scrambled up on the rock and, running along the lines from side to side like a typewriter roller when you press the keys, he began to read.

'Dear Wilberforce,' he began, 'We are on our holidays in Scotland and the weather is lovely beautiful warm water and really fat cuttlefish would you like to come and stay with me? I do hope you can come send me a postcard to say yes and let me know when you expect to arrive from your loving Aunty Barnacle.'

Wilberforce reared up on his tail and shouted. 'Hooray! Aunty Barnacle's asked me to Scotland. Hoots!' Then he did a complete swishing circle with a swirl that quite knocked Nelson off his rock on top of Melody who had already been swept flat on the sand.

'Ah luv a lassie,
A bonny heelan' lassie,
Tiddle-om-pom-ti-iddle-omty-pom,
Tiddle-om-pom the heather . . .'

Wilberforce was swimming loop-the-loops and uncontrolled banked turns of joy as he sang:

'The bonny, heelan' heather . . .'

'What on earth's all that about?' asked Nelson, picking himself up.

'It's Scots wha hae, ye wee, mickle, sassenachy crabby,' shouted Wilberforce, settling down again, but still obviously excited.

'There's a P.S.,' said Nelson.

'A bit more?'

'That's it, and it says, "P.S.".'

'It said that before.'

'No it didn't, *I* said that. It says, "P.S. If you have any young friend you would like with you, *do* bring them too."'

'Melody,' cried Wilberforce at once, 'would you like to come?'

'Oh, thank you, Wilberforce! Is it nice at your Aunty Barnacle's?'

'My dear, shrimpy friend,' replied Wilberforce, 'my Aunty Barnacle's the tops, the utmost, the absolute, the ultimate. Extra treats, you know,' he sighed, 'and no bed time,' he added with rapture, eyes closed . . . 'And rides and visits,' and an even more rapt look came over his face, 'and surreptitious fifty penny pieces slipped into the fin, and teas with sea pie,' he added in ecstasy, 'and grub generally . . . Oh, yes, it's *nice* visiting Aunty Barnacle's.'

'Hooray, hooray!
We're going away!
Wilberforce's Aunty Barnacle has asked us to stay.'

'That doesn't go properly,' said Wilberforce.
'There are too many words at the end.'

'I know,' said Melody, 'but I'm far too excited to bother with fiddly bits like how many
words there are. When are we off?'

Now all this while a sort of droopy look was
coming over Nelson's face; a sort of 'I'm-being-
missed-out-sort-of-a-look', a sort of 'Haven't-
I-been-forgotten-sort-of-a-look,' a sort of 'I'm-
not-wanted-here-sort-of-a-look,' and he started
to sidle sideways with dragging feet. For-
tunately, Wilberforce, who was very kind-
hearted, saw at once.

'Oh, Nelson,' he said, 'whatever's up with
you, my cretaceous, carapaceous and totally
crab-like little companion. Did you think we
were going to leave you out? You must come
too.'

'But the P.S. only says, "if you have *a* friend,"
and *I* should make two,' answered Nelson half
hopefully, half in tears.

'But after that it says, "bring *them* too",
which means any number.'

'But wouldn't Mrs Barnacle mind?'

'My Aunty Barnacle is the most hospitable
aunty in the whole of the Western Isles, where

she lives, and when I write and tell her I want to bring *two* friends, she'll be *doubly* pleased. Will you come?'

'Oh, Wilberforce, thank you so much!' And a tear of pure joy rolled down the tip of one of Nelson's feelers. Then he began a most peculiar little figure-of-eight crab dance with all his eight legs together looking as if they were doing a sort of complicated multiple knitting, until they got so in the way of each other that he collapsed laughing on the sand.

'When do we start?' cried Melody.

'Tomorrow,' said Wilberforce. 'But now I must write that letter to Aunty telling her when we shall be there.' And with four powerful flips of his fluke-tail—per-roosh, per-roosh, per-roosh, per-roosh!—Wilberforce disappeared round a great boulder.

'I'd better go and pack,' said Melody, and —pitcherpoop!—she disappeared into her cave.

'Oh well,' said Nelson, 'me too!' And he scuttled back round the bank of red leaf-weed.

2

A Narrow Escape

It really was *the* most glorious day; just the day to start a visit. Outside Melody's cave, shafts of light danced through the crystal water to stipple the sandy sea-bed with wavering lozenges of sapphire, silver and gold.

Full of excitement, Melody was packing her vanity case (the one with the initials M.S., for Melody Shrimp, on the outside). On the top she put a packet of seaweed sandwiches, two of the green sort and one of the red, and tucked away below was her favourite piece of branching pink coral from the shelf of ornaments. She had only just clicked the catch, when a familiar voice rumbled through the cave-mouth from the open sea.

'Ahoy, and avast, and belay there, ye lazy lubber! The train standing at platform two-and-a-half will leave yesterday for the Western Isles calling at Rockall, Ushant, Clapham Junction and Kirby Bellars. Please fasten your safety belts, and hand your disembarkation tickets to the station-master without delay!'

Pitcherpoop!—Melody was outside the cave before she realised she had started to move.

'Wilberforce, you old silly,' she cried, 'you *do* talk a lot of nonsense.'

'I don't care,' laughed the whale with a grin twice as wide as usual, 'I'm on holiday!'

'And so am I,' put in Nelson, the crab, scuttling round from Wilberforce's further side. 'Isn't it exciting, Melody!'

'Oh yes, yes, yes,' cried Melody. 'When do we start?'

'Forthwith, now, or a little sooner, if you like,' laughed Wilberforce. 'Just hang your luggage on board, and we'll be off.' And he pointed to a small three-pronged kedge-anchor which he had fastened by its chain to one of his fins. Nelson's carpet-bag was already hanging there, so Melody put her vanity case on another of the prongs with the initials, M.S., on the outside, and off they went.

'But where's your luggage, Wilberforce?' asked Melody.

'I am correctly dressed,' replied Wilberforce, indicating a plaid tam-o'-shanter cocked jauntily on one side of his vast forehead, 'and that is all you need, when visiting my Aunty Barnacle.'

Melody almost gave way to a giggle at the

sight of the bright red and green pimple of a
hat on such a huge head, but she managed to
turn it into a sneeze so as not to hurt her
friend's feelings.

'I have also,' said Wilberforce, nodding to a
neat little bundle tied up in a clean white
napkin which hung on the third prong of the
kedge-anchor, 'I have also taken precautions
against shortage, lack, er-general deficiency not
to say tragedy,' and his eyes took on a serious
and deeply worried look, 'in case the supply of
cuttlefish should not be as plentiful en route
as might be desired.'

'I thought you were supposed to be on a diet

for your figure,' said Melody with a very straight face and a barely perceptible twinkle in her eye.

'Whales who eat a lot more food,
Than a slim whale really should,
Find a vast increase of weight
Is their inevitable fate!'

'I don't much like your rhyming food with should,' said Wilberforce with an equally barely perceptible twinkle in his eye. 'Besides, one has to keep up one's strength for the journey, hasn't one?' And he burst into song:

'I'll tak the high road,
An' ye'll tak the low . . .
       Oh,
A life on the ocean wave,
Terumperty-umpty-um,
A life on the umpty . . .

Good morning, Mrs Whiting, we're just off to Scotland . . . Yes, to see my Aunty Barnacle . . . Good-bye, Stella! . . . Hallo there, Mr Gar! . . . Yes, that's right! . . . Oh, I expect we shall be away at least three weeks . . .'

All their friends and acquaintances seemed to be up and about, and wishing them a happy holiday and calm seas on the way. Nelson scuttered along the bottom, and Wilberforce pushed on with powerful thrusts of his great tail—per-rump-ah, per-rump-ah—and Melody flashed and darted by his side—pfut-pfut-pfut.

But presently the 'pfut-pfut' became 'pfut-ha, pfut-pfut-a-ha, pfut-a-ha-a-ha, er pfut-ha-pfut-ha, a-ha, a-ha, a-ha!' Until at last, 'Wilberforce!' called Melody. 'Could we stop, a-ha, a-ha, for a bit, a-ha, a-ha, a-ha, do you think, please?'

'But of course, my little dot, my tiny chip, my little mite of shrimpiness; what is it?'

'Wilberforce, a-ha, a-ha, a-ha, how far is it to Scotland?'

'Four or five days' good swimming!'

'Four or five days! . . . But I'm out of breath already, you're going so fast!'

'Me too,' wailed Nelson, limping up, and the corners of his little mouth were beginning to droop, though he was manfully controlling himself. 'And I've got a blister coming already on the third foot on my right side.'

'There!' said Wilberforce, 'how thoughtless of me; I had forgotten that you and Nelson were so—er vest-pocket, er portable, so miniature; whilst old Wilberforce is rather more like the gasworks, bulky, voluminous, er bigger! . . . Now, let me think! . . . But of course,' he brightened up, 'didn't I say it myself!— You're *portable!* What we'll do is this: I'll swim up to the surface, and I'll open my mouth wide and fill the bottom half with water for you, Melody, my tiny wee minchin, to swim in, and Nelson can swim there too, or ride on the top of my head.'

'Oh, good!' cried Nelson.

So Wilberforce floated quietly up to the surface — blubble-ubble-obble-obble-ibble-ebble-abble-abble-sfisch!—and Melody and Nelson 'went aboard'.

'I shall call this "the cabin",' said Melody swimming round in the little pool Wilberforce had made for her.

'And I shall call this "the bridge",' said Nelson very proudly from the top of Wilberforce's tam-o'-shanter.

So off they went—per-roosh, per-roosh, per-roosh—very comfortably because the sea was quite calm. And Melody found that by swimming right to the front of the cabin and popping up her little black boot-button eyes as far as they would go, she could see everything as they went along.

The sky was real blue-blue with hardly a cloud in sight, and two steamers passed in quick succession. One had passengers on, who waved to them, and the other was a stubby little tramp that gave two hoots on its siren—hoop-hoop! Melody was enchanted.

'It's just like going on a voyage in a big ocean liner,' she cried, and broke into one of her snatches:

'For a summer cruise
You couldn't choose
Better than sail
In *The Wilberforce Whale*.'

Wilberforce laughed. 'I like the sentiment, and thank you very kindly,' he said.

Just then they found themselves overhauling a very smart gold and white pleasure yacht, which began to put on speed as they drew level.

'Go on, Wilberforce,' said Nelson from the bridge, 'don't let them beat you. Step on it a bit!'

So Wilberforce began to speed up—per-rump-ah, per-rump-ah, per-rump-ah, per-rump-ah, per-rump-ah—and his great fluke-tail went up and down in the water faster and faster.

'Go on! Go on!' shouted Nelson.

A bow wave started to build up in front of the vast jaw, till Melody was afraid she might be washed away. But the race was on, and all three were far too interested to see themselves inching up on the sleek, sporty vessel to think about anything else.

'Faster, faster!' cried Nelson.

Gradually they pulled level, and the whale had a foaming wake behind him as he swam with all his might. The yacht was well over on their port bow, and all eyes were turned that way to watch as Wilberforce started to get his nose in front. Then, suddenly, Melody shrieked:

'Stop, Wilberforce, stop! There's nets ahead!'

Alas, it was all too true. To port was the yacht, to starboard, unnoticed until this instant, a large trawler, and stretching from it on a line of bobbing floats, a massive deep-sea seine-net. What to do? No turning to either quarter because of the other craft, and they were already too near to the net for Wilberforce at full power and speed to stop before he would get caught and hopelessly entangled in it!

'Inside both!' snapped Wilberforce, because although he was quite an easy-going old fuddy-duddy in ordinary, everyday life, when it came to a crisis, he was remarkably decisive.

Melody and Nelson were hardly safe inside before Wilberforce snapped his great jaws tight closed. It was pitch dark, and they felt him turn sharply downwards and sound in a vertical dive to the bottom. It was so steep and fast that the two little animals found themselves pinned to the roof of the whale's mouth with half their breath knocked out of them, and Melody's ears 'popped', so swiftly did they go down. Then the dive levelled off and they both slid, half rolling, onto the floor again. For a moment, Wilberforce lay on the bottom. Then very gingerly he opened his mouth, and his two passengers stepped out.

'Look!' said Wilberforce nodding his head astern. Melody's eyes followed his. A short distance behind, the great net was being dragged in by the trawler. It hung only ten or twelve feet clear of the bottom, and Wilberforce must almost have grazed it as he passed under.

'Phew!' said Wilberforce, 'phew! Crikey-go-lightly and tickle-me-toenails! No more speeding for me without looking where I'm going!'

Nelson dragged out his carpet-bag. 'I think we ought to pitch camp for the night,' he said, scuttling inside it.

'I thought that was your luggage,' said Melody.

'Oh, no, it's my tent,' said Nelson.

So the others agreed. And some moments later, Wilberforce said:

'We'll take it more carefully tomorrow.'

'More carefully tomorrow,' agreed Melody. Then two little eyes popped out of the carpet-bag, and, 'Me too!' said Nelson.

3

The Black-headed Gull

The next day was bright and sparkling as ever, and Melody, Nelson and Wilberforce swam on comfortably until about half past twelve, when the great whale murmured one word, 'Luncheon!' and dived suddenly—blabble-abble-ebble-ibble-obble-obble-ubble-ubble-oomf — down to the bottom of the sea. Melody and Nelson climbed out of the cabin and took all the luggage off the kedge-anchor.

Then murmuring, 'I think I spotted a promising crevice for cuttlefish,' Wilberforce gave one terrific push—per-roosh—with his fluke-tail and disappeared among some very thick Sea Whistle weed. The whale's stroke was so powerful that it caught Melody and Nelson and all the baggage in a whirlpool, so that they and their belongings were swept round and round, upside down and right way up, and quite powerless to save themselves, until the swirling eddy steadied and settled full half a minute later.

'I *do* wish Wilberforce would remember how strong he is,' wailed Melody straightening out her feelers and antennae which had become all tangled up. Then she and Nelson sat down to their own lunch, sharing Nelson's sandwiches as they had eaten Melody's the day before. Then they tried playing 'tig', but Melody was far too fast for Nelson. So they changed to 'hide-and-seek', which was much more fun because everywhere was new and there were lots and lots of rocks with caves and crannies. At last they sat down quite breathless, and Nelson said:

'What's the time?'

And Melody said:

'Where's Wilberforce?'

'He's been away *hours*,' said Nelson. 'Do you think he's lost?'

'Nothing as big as Wilberforce could possibly get lost,' said Melody, 'but perhaps we ought to go and see if anything has happened to him.'

'But we're very small,' said Nelson, and his voice was beginning to get a little quavery; 'we're not big like Wilberforce, *we* might lose our way!'

So they decided to shout as loud as possible, and both began together:

'Wilberforce! . . . Wilberfor-orce! . . . *Wilber-force!*'

After the third call there was a disturbance in the distance among the Sea Whistle weed, and very slowly and leisurely, Wilberforce's vast bulk eased into view. But it was a rather altered Wilberforce. His face was puffed; his beady eyes seemed to have sunk into two saucers of fat; his breathing was heavy; and his whole body seemed slightly swollen.

'Ah-h-h-h!' he sighed, settling on the sea-bed. 'What's the trouble?'

'We thought you were lost,' said Melody.

'Lost! Oh certainly not, just round the corner.'

'But what *have* you been doing all this time?'

'Nothing!'

'Nothing?'

'Well, just luncheon!'

'Luncheon! All this time!'

'One of the pleasures of holidaying in foreign parts is the strange and novel cuisine, and the cuttlefish . . .'

'Wilberforce! How many helpings?'

'The er—cuttlefish were so fat, so chubby, so exquisitely plump . . .'

'How many helpings, Wilberforce?'

'And so delicately flavoured; such essence, such verve!'

'How many, Wilberforce?'

'Er . . . five!'

'FIVE helpings of cuttlefish!' cried Melody. 'However are you going to be able to swim on this afternoon?'

'Well,' said Wilberforce, 'I *was* considering a little nap . . . ah-h-h, . . . so tender! . . . such variety! . . . such succulence! . . . such hic!' said Wilberforce, and then, 'Oh crikey!' And then again, 'Hic! Pardon!' said Wilberforce, 'Hic!'

'Wilberforce,' said Melody severely, 'you're a disgrace! You have *five* helpings of cuttlefish, and your tum's so full you can't swim a stroke and now you've got hiccups! I'm ashamed of you! What *are* we going to do with him?' She turned to Nelson.

'They say patting on the back's helpful,' said Nelson, and he clambered up on the great whale, and began to jump up and down. But all that happened was that Wilberforce started to giggle.

'Huh-huh-huh,' he gurgled, 'hic! Don't do that, you're tick-hic-ickling me! Hic—Oh bother!' And the last 'hic' was so violent that it shot the little crab several feet up onto a rocky ledge, where a limpet was so surprised at his sudden arrival that he stuck himself—plup!— firmly back on the rocky face.

'Try standing on your head,' suggested Melody, 'they say that helps.'

And rather unwillingly Wilberforce reared up his great fluke-tail—ber-lob, . . . ber-lob, . . . ber-lob—until he was balanced head downwards like a gigantic tadpole. For some seconds he hung there in complete silence.

'There!' said Melody. 'What did I tell you?'

'Good,' said Wilberforce, 'you're quite right, I'm . . . hic!'

'Oh bother!' said Melody.

'Oh hic!' replied Wilberforce.

'Human beings,' said Nelson, 'sip a glass of water.'

'But we're sea creatures, and we live in it,' said Wilberforce.

'Perhaps if *they* cure it with a sip of water, *we* could cure it with a bubble of air.'

'I'll try anything,' groaned Wilberforce. 'I feel like a balloon that's been filled with lead.'

So Melody picked a leaf of Bladderlocks and swam up with it to the surface, where she trailed it behind her, gathering air on the underside. Then she took the two ends of the leaf, one in each pincer, and pulled down so that the seaweed made a sort of parachute with the airbubble trapped at the top. But the trouble is that airbubbles float *up,* and Melody wanted to go *down,* and the bubble was stronger than she was. So she pulled and tugged and dived and struggled, but try how she would, she couldn't get it to budge an inch.

Then suddenly, something sharp came down through the water and went 'snap' just a hair's breadth from her tail. Her feelers stood on end with horror. It was a black-headed gull, looking for dinner, and dinner was Melody!

'Help! Help!' she gasped. Pfut-pfut, pitter-fut, pitter-fut—and she started to swim in several directions all at once. Now, of course, if the poor little thing had had the sense to let go of the seaweed and dive, she would have been quite safe from the greedy bird, but in her panic she only clung on tighter, darting in consternation from side to side—pfut-pfut— 'Help!'—pitter-fut, pitter-fut, pitter-fut— 'Help! Wilberforce!—pitter-fut, pitter-fut— 'Nelson, Wilberforce, Help!' and over and over again the horrible black-headed gull dived into the water and tried to snap her up. But the Bladderlocks covered her so that he couldn't see exactly where to pounce. He missed and missed again, but each time he seemed to be getting a little nearer. Then suddenly there was a terrific swirl—perrablompf!—and everything went black as night.

'Oh dear, I've been eaten by a seagull!' cried Melody; 'Oh dear, I've been eaten by a seagull! Oh dear, . . .' and then she paused; 'It isn't particularly uncomfortable being

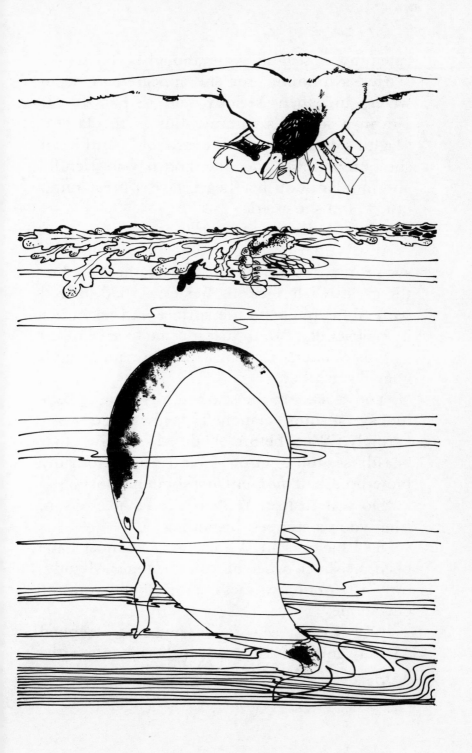

eaten by a seagull,' she thought. Then she started swimming, for she appeared to be in water, and then Melody said to herself, 'If I'm in a seagull's tummy, this is the largest seagull's tum I've ever heard of.' And then she bumped into the side, and it was friendly and familiar, and her heart gave a great jump of joy, and she cried,

'Wilberforce, let me out!'

And Wilberforce opened his mouth, and she swam out free at the bottom of the sea. For the great whale, hearing her cries, had lunged with all his might to the surface and taken her in his friendly mouth just in time to save her.

'Oh Wilberforce, has the horrid seagull gone?' she asked.

'You're safe on the sea-bed, my little mipsy-mopsy shrimp,' laughed Wilberforce reassuringly. 'But before I dived, I gave that beastly seagull a jet of air and water from my blow-hole, and *that* sent *him* about his business.'

'Do you realize, Wilberforce,' said Nelson, 'that you've stopped hiccuping?'

'So I have,' said Wilberforce, 'it must have been the shock of seeing you in danger Melody, my little minnow messmate; thank you for curing me.'

'And thank *you* for saving *me*,' replied Melody and burst into one of her chants with:

'Who is the champion, can you guess,
That saves poor damsels in distress,
(Ever so brave and ever so strong),
The knightly hero of my song?

Clad in a coat of shining mail,
(A paragon of the House of Whale),
Who fights all evil, rights all wrong,
Who is the hero of my song?

Who is the hero of the day?
Who is the subject of my lay?
See where he comes on prancing horse,
Sir Galahad Wilberforce, of course!'

And Wilberforce replied laughing, 'Huh-huh-huh! I should look pretty funny trying to ride a *sea*horse, eh? Huh-huh!' and he blushed ever so slightly. 'Well,' he continued, 'I feel better now. Shall we go on with the journey?'

4

The Regatta

Nelson awoke. There was a noise in the distance — perlomp-erlomp-erlomp-erlomp. 'That's a fishing boat with a diesel engine,' he thought, and cautiously poked two eyes and two feelers out of his carpet-bag. The boat was bearing down towards him. Nelson lay quite, quite still; boats were generally harmless to crabs, but you never knew! The engine slipped into neutral—limpy-impy-impy-impy-imp. 'It's going to stop,' thought Nelson, and almost at once, the whining reverse gear brought it to a halt—ying-ying-ying-ying-ying-ying. Then the engine cut and the boat lay directly over him.

A moment later, down over the side came an anchor on a hawser which was paid steadily out until it landed three or four paces from Nelson's carpet-bag. The anchor lay with its flukes on the sea-bed. Somebody up above gave a testing pull on the hawser. The anchor shifted slightly and then engaged partly in the sand and partly under a rock. Then there was a splash on the surface, and looking up with his stalk-like eyes, Nelson saw that the hawser was fastened not to a boat, but to a sort of upside-down cone painted red.

The boat started up, turned round and disappeared the way it had come—perlomp-erlomp-erlomp-erlomp-erlomp-erlomp. For some seconds after the engine had died away Nelson did not stir. Then, very cautiously, he put out two more claws, then two more, and finally with timid looks darting to either side, he drew his whole body clear of his little carpet-bag home. Then he moved with his quaint sideways scuttle at a safe distance and on the very tips of his little claws right round the strange anchor, its hawser and the peculiar red thing at the surface, and he didn't feel at all sure about any of it.

'It looks like a buoy,' he said. Then, 'Melody,' he called, 'are you awake?'

Melody's two longest feelers appeared above the sand where she had buried herself for the night.

'Oh, *do* hurry up,' called Nelson, and then as the rest of her appeared he added, 'look!'

Melody looked enquiringly at the anchor, the hawser and the strange object above, and swam round it once, a little nearer than

Nelson had done but still at a safe distance.

'A boat brought it just now,' added Nelson. 'What do you think it is?'

'It's a buoy, I think,' said Melody, 'but it *could* be a mine.'

'Oh-oh, that would blow us all up,' quavered the little crab. 'I do hope it isn't; hadn't we better go and see Wilberforce about it?'

Wilberforce was resting on a deep bed of sea grass.

'Are you awake?' asked Melody.

'No!' said Wilberforce.

'Oh, do be sensible! There's something you ought to look at.'

Wilberforce paddled over. He looked at the anchor, he looked at the hawser and he looked at the conical red thing at the top.

'That, my little pippity pals, my tiddly chums, my tiny cronies, that is a buoy. It marks something, probably a wreck.'

'Well, they put it down by me, and I'm not a wreck,' said Nelson indignantly.

'Well, perhaps it marks a treasure trove,' said Wilberforce.

'I can't see any pirates' chest,' said Melody looking round hopefully.

'Well, it marks something, mark my words,' said Wilberforce. 'Let's have breakfast.'

So they did that, looking up from time to

time at the strange buoy, which floated silently and unconcernedly above. Then they tidied their camp away so that nobody could ever tell they had been there, as all good campers should.

They had just hung the last of the luggage on Wilberforce's kedge-anchor, when there was a sharp hissing sound—fiss-iss-iss-iss— and towards them over their heads slid the keel of a small racing dinghy.

The waterline was red with black below, and up to the gunnel she was white, for she was heeling so hard over that the whole of the lee beam was under water—Fiss-iss-iss-iss— she came on, swiftly knifing the sea. She reached the buoy and rounded it with a lurch and a crack as the sails jibbed across and refilled with wind. With upturned heads they watched her go about as two other dinghies appeared coming up on the same tack, one with a yellow keel and mahogany sides, the other green all over, and they too slid round the buoy as Wilberforce shouted with excitement:

'It's a marker buoy for a regatta; look, they're racing!'

So they quickly swam a little way off so as not to come up under the boats, and Wilberforce surfaced — blubble-obbl-ibble-abble-sfisch! — with Melody in the cabin and Nelson on the bridge.

Wilberforce was right; under a pale blue sky with chasing clouds a regatta was in full swing. They were a little distance off a promenade hung with bunting, and boats were everywhere: slim yachts moored at a jetty; little white motor-boats with gentlemen in sailing rig moving importantly about, and white and shiny cruisers, very opulent and dressed over all with flags. And then there were the racing boats with blue sails and red sails and yellow and black striped sails, and just beautiful plain white wing-like sails. The small scudding dinghies which had passed over them earlier were returning to land in the distance like a cloud of equatorial butterflies, standing over on their sides as if they would capsize at any moment. Suddenly there was a loud bang.

'Oh,' cried Melody, startled. 'What was that?'

'Just the starting gun,' answered Wilberforce; 'they go off whenever a race starts or ends.'

And out through the crowd of dinghies came a heavier class of racer with bigger sails leaning splendidly into the white horses of the choppy waves, carving their way rapidly out towards them.

For a moment they just gaped. Then the questions flooded:

'What's he going that way for? Why doesn't he steer straight?' Nelson and Melody almost shouted each other down. 'Isn't that pink sail pretty! How do they stop going if the wind blows all the time? What does that flag with the blue and white check mean?' and finally; 'How do you know when anybody wins?'

There was such a stream of questions, that Wilberforce for a moment just floated there and laughed.

'You can't understand a thing as complicated as a sailing race all in a breath, my mites, my chickadees, my little midget mariners,' he said. 'You have to do a bit yourself first.'

So they just sat back and started to enjoy everything without in the least being really sure of what was happening, though Wilberforce did point out the finishing line between two distant buoys.

In some mysterious way, Wilberforce had exchanged his tam-o-shanter for a white nautical cap, which he had at a very jaunty angle, and made Melody want to giggle again. And in no time at all, the whale had become a sort of grandstand. First of all, an old lobster and his wife—*very* pleasant people who had been sent South for their health by their doctor —asked if they might join Nelson on the bridge *most* politely; and then a very jolly young person, a Mrs Sprat with two twin daughters, asked to be allowed to join Melody in the cabin. And eventually four seagulls, whom nobody liked very much (particularly Melody who felt distinctly nervous after her last experience with the Black-head) came and perched on Wilberforce's back with the barest 'keek-keek' to ask permission. But nobody had the heart to turn them off.

Then the race was on them, first by one and two, then all in a crowd. Among these was a large black yacht with an arrogant curve to its prow, and the name *Pirate* on its side. It was captained by a large man with a black moustache, a red face and a very loud and bullying voice. He seemed to be very angry.

'Water!' he yelled at the nearest boat, as he rounded the buoy. 'Give way, man, don't you know the rules!' And then to the next boat, 'Can't you see I'm on the port tack? Give way, man! I'll lodge a complaint!'

Pirate seemed to be elbowing her way through the crowd of boats in a most rude and unpleasant manner. Then the red-faced sailorman caught sight of Wilberforce.

'Whales on the course! Disgraceful! Ought to be got rid of! I shall tell the committee.'

'Well, I certainly hope *he* doesn't win, whoever else does,' said Melody.

'Me too,' added Nelson.

Just then another yacht passed called *Speedwell*. She was all white and gold with a blue sail. An elderly man was at the tiller, and a lady and two young fellows were working the sails. They seemed to be thoroughly enjoying the race.

'Just look at the whale basking with the seagulls perched on him,' said the lady.

'He's got a friendly face,' said one of the young men. 'Look, he's positively smiling at us.'

'A whale means good luck,' said the man at the helm, and all four waved at Wilberforce.

'Bring us luck!' they called.

'That's the boat for me,' said Melody. 'Go on, *Speedwell!*'

The boats went twice round the course, and soon it was clear that *Pirate* and *Speedwell* were pulling ahead of all the others. On the last leg, though *Speedwell* was overhauling *Pirate,* the rude and red-faced sailorman was still ahead by a cable.

'Oh, go on *Speedwell,*' called everyone on the 'grandstand'; 'don't let that wretched *Pirate* win.'

But although the gap between them was closing it was clear that it was not closing quickly enough. And everyone was just watching and hoping for the impossible, when suddenly Wilberforce said:

'I am going to take a little swim . . . Yes,' he said meditatively, 'I think a little swim will do us all good. Please clear the decks.'

So despite some disappointment, Nelson came down into the cabin, and the other guests disembarked as Wilberforce dived, not too deep, and had a little swim—perlumpf-perlumpf—and after they had swum a short while—perlumpf-perlumpf—there was the tiniest sensation, the minutest suggestion of a shudder or jar or 'pfumpf' as if they had grazed something in passing.

Shortly afterwards they resurfaced. And just as Wilberforce opened his mouth so that they could see, the finishing gun went 'bang', and over the line sailed *Speedwell* taut and trim, to the cheers of all the onlookers.

'But where's *Pirate?*' asked Melody.

'Well, I'm not sure,' replied Wilberforce, 'but I'm afraid he seems to have had a bit of bad luck, because just as he was going to cross the finishing line, his rudder hit some submerged object or other,' and Wilberforce's tummy began to heave and shake like a jelly as if he was trying to smother a laugh, 'and got stuck so he couldn't steer, and he went the wrong side of a buoy and got disqualified.' The laughter was now beyond suppression; Wilberforce was laughing outright, 'huh-huh-huh-huh-huh! Look, he's going in circles.'

And they looked, and *Pirate* was going round and round in circles with the rude and red-faced sailorman saying some very rude things indeed. Then it struck a sand bank, and the sail came down with a 'wump', and then all they could see was a billowing mass of sail cloth and two angry arms gesticulating.

'You cunning old thing!' said Melody.

'What have I done?' said Wilberforce.

Melody chanted:

'Oh, Wilberforce Whale,

You make me turn pale,
At your depth of deceit.
You wicked old cheat!'

'I think, my little shrimpy pal, my little crabby playmate,' said Wilberforce, 'I think, perhaps, we ought to be moving,' and he started to dive.

'But I'm glad you did it,' said Melody just as they finally submerged.

5

The Wreck and the Mariner

They swam away from the shore out to the open sea most of the day, with Wilberforce surfacing to breathe from time to time. There was still a chuckle in his voice as he thought of the rather naughty trick he had played at the regatta.

'Poetic justice, my little cracker-crab,' he said to Nelson; 'served him right, pure poetic justice!' Then he burst into one of his rumbling songs:

> 'Oh, I do like to be beside the seaside;
>> I do like to be beside the sea,
> Where the om-tiddly-om goes
>> Pom-tiddly . . .

Bother! I've forgotten the words.'

'You always forget the words,' said Melody.

'Oh, that doesn't matter; it's the lilt and swing that sends me,' said Wilberforce. 'I'm feeling great—a perfect example of poetic justice. Huh, huh, huh!' he gurgled.

Generally they kept near the bottom so that

Nelson could scuttle along by himself, while Melody also left the cabin for a little swim. Pfut-pfut-pfut—she went quite leisurely, and —per-rump-ah, per-rump-ah, per-rump-ah— went Wilberforce keeping pace, and it was all very comfortable and a nice change. And as Wilberforce said, *he* had no objection to carrying them on board, but it *did* make talking difficult. Well, have *you* ever tried making sensible conversation with a shrimp swimming round in your mouth and a crab balanced on your head?

Late in the afternoon they decided to stop for the day. They unhooked the luggage from Wilberforce's kedge-anchor, and after he had laid out his carpet-bag, Nelson scuttled about doing a little scavenging for supper, whilst Melody nibbled a leaf or two of fresh seaweed. For once Wilberforce said he wasn't hungry, and very soon they were all three lying head to stream snug and friendly on the sea-bed.

'Tell us about your Aunty Barnacle,' said Nelson.

'Well, she isn't a real aunty,' said Wilberforce, 'just a very close family friend. Her real name is Arabella, Arabella Barnacle. We call her Aunty Barnacle to show that she's an *adopted* aunty, if you know what I mean.'

'Yes, of course,' said Melody; 'I've got one of those myself.'

'And she's a hundred and two feet long.'

'A whale a hundred and two feet long!' gasped Nelson.

'Oh, she isn't a whale,' said Wilberforce; 'she's a . . . she's a . . . well I don't know . . . she's a family friend. She has a huge long tail, a lumpy body with four flippers and then quite a small head on a very long neck, which she sticks out of the water when she wants to know what's going on, and she breathes air like me.'

'Does she look fierce?' asked Nelson.

'Oh no, she has a *kind* face,' said Wilberforce, 'except when she wears her spectacles, which make her look rather strict. She has to wear spectacles because there is so little light at the depth she lives. And she is immensely rich,' he continued. 'She has two homes, one deep in the Atlantic Ocean, while for holidays she has a little place in a Scottish loch. She spends a lot of her time knitting seaweed comforters for distressed mariners, and she *adores* jelly babies. Remind me, Nelson, my little crab crony, to get you to go to a sweet shop as soon as we are near enough inshore. I always bring my aunty a packet of jelly babies or winter mixture according to season; she adores them both . . . And she's a Celt.'

'What's a Celt?' asked Melody.

'The sort of a person who lives in those sort of a parts, my jiminy shrimp,' replied the whale. 'They have second sight, you know, they can see the future, and they can *do* things!'

'Do things!'

'Yes.'

'What sort of things?'

'Well, these hats of mine—you may have noticed . . .'

Melody giggled.

'Well, she taught me how to make them out of nothing—a rune, you know.'

'A rune?'

'A charm.'

'A rune to make hats! Oh do make a hat!' cried Nelson.

'Shut your eyes tight,' said Wilberforce, 'and no cheating. If you look while I'm doing it, I shan't be able to make another change till the next quarter of the moon.'

So Melody and Nelson shut their eyes tight as tight as tight, and Wilberforce began to mutter:

'Tongue of toad and wing of bat,
Make a new and natty hat.'

'. . . something appropriate,' he added, concentrating very hard—u-mm-mm-mm-mm! Then there was a 'ching' like a little bell, and

Wilberforce said, 'You can look now.' And there he was balancing a natty little deerstalker right in the middle of his head. 'In case Aunty Barnacle invites us for a day on the moors,' he said.

'You are silly,' laughed Melody.

'Do the flaps come down?' asked Nelson.

'Of course,' replied Wilberforce, 'it's a real one.'

Melody chanted:

> 'For the funniest hats
> You will ever see fish in
> Take Wilberforce Whale,
> The master magician.'

'I will forgive you your horrid rhyme,' laughed Wilberforce, 'but I insist I am *not* a fish.'

'Do it again,' cried Nelson.

'Oh, please!' exclaimed Melody.

And while they shut their eyes, Wilberforce muttered again:

> 'Tongue of toad and wing of bat,
> Make a new and natty hat.'

' . . . something a little unusual,' he added with renewed concentration. Then there was the tiny 'ching' as before, and there he was resplendent in a ducal coronet all ermine and gold and strawberry leaves.

'Lovely!' cried Melody, and Nelson clapped

his front pincers.

'Thank you, my little fishy fans, my crustaceous little claque,' laughed Wilberforce.

'Do it again!' said Nelson.

But before Wilberforce could say another word, there was a 's-s-swoosh, s-s-swoosh, s-s-swoosh,' and a simply huge racing hull with a very deep keel passed right over their heads, and then another, and then another—s-s-swoosh, s-s-swoosh—carving the surface of a sea that seemed a good deal rougher than earlier that day.

'Those are the big fellows from the regatta,' said Wilberforce. 'The deep sea stuff, out for two or three days. You just watch them for a moment while I change into something more comfortable,' and the next time the two little friends looked at the whale, he was wearing a sensible, woolly knitted seaman's hat in navy blue with a white pom-pom on top.

The intervals between the boats increased, and then one came over that was quite a long way behind. Just as it was right above their heads it gave a sudden shudder, and there was a sort of twanging sound like a violin string breaking. Then the boat stood almost still, wallowing on an even keel, and it started to drift sideways.

'Looks as if he's lost a stay,' said Wilberforce. 'Let's go up and see; he may be in trouble.'

What a different scene greeted them as they surfaced! The sea, so still below, was building into greasy, green rollers, while heavy black clouds were racing across the sky over a wind that shouted and whistled as it broke the wave crests into flying white spume. The yacht, a big one, was clearly disabled. Wilberforce was right, a stay had given and the mast was in danger. The crew had the mainsail down, and she was trying to weather a small islet under the storm jib, but she was clearly being driven by the wind onto a lee shore and would never make it. The friends watched horrified as she grounded only a minute or two later. Five of the crew jumped into shallow water, and waded with great difficulty onto the rocky shore, but the jar of striking overbalanced one man into the water on the seaward side. He was wearing a bright yellow buoyancy jacket, and the three friends could already see the rescue launch coming back in the distance to help them. It was a sorry sight with the broken yacht being pounded by the waves.

'Let's go down, my little mates,' said Wilberforce. 'I hate to see a good ship hurt, but the rescue launch is there, so at least the crew will be all right.'

So rather sadly they returned to camp in the stillness of the deep water. There they lay not talking for some minutes, just listening to the engines of the rescue craft—prum-prum-prum-prum—by the wreck.

'He's taking a long time to get the crew off,' said Wilberforce as the engine continued running. The boat seemed to be going in circles.

'He's searching for something,' said Wilberforce.

Then Melody called, 'Look!'

Above their heads floated the legs of a sailor in a yellow buoyancy jacket. He was treading water rapidly to keep afloat and warm, and he was obviously being swept out to sea on a race tide.

'It's a totally deserted and distressed mariner,' cried Nelson, very disturbed.

'That's what they're searching for,' said Wilberforce. 'They don't realise how far the tide has carried him, and it's getting dark; they'll miss him! I must do something! You two stay right here!' And the great whale lunged for the surface—per-roosh!

The weather had freshened further, and the rescue boat was searching half a mile in the wrong direction. Wilberforce looked about him. There were jagged waves everywhere, and the light was failing fast. Then he noticed that the yacht's dinghy had broken from its davits and was floating upright, held only by a fouled line. With all his power he made for the now deserted yacht. The painter hung over the dinghy's side. Taking it in his mouth he pushed and twisted and jostled and pulled, being careful not to capsize the craft, until suddenly it freed itself from the line. Then, with a series of mighty strokes from his powerful fluke-tail—per-rump-ah, per-rump-ah, per-rump-ah—he set about towing it out to sea to where he knew the sailor would be.

He stopped some yards short of the man, where he couldn't be seen, for fear of frighten-

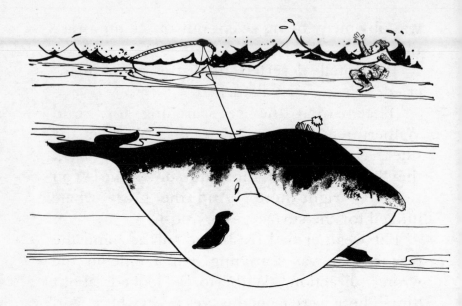

ing him. Then he released the dinghy and let it float to him on the surface. Wilberforce stood off several yards and watched.

As soon as he saw the boat, the man's face lit up. He swam with new strength to grip the transom and climb over the stern. For a moment he sat there gathering his breath. Then he reached into a locker, took out a sort of pistol, and pointed it at the sky. There was a sharp report, and—fisz-sz-sz-sz—up went the signal. Then two bright red stars exploded reflecting red on the cloud. Instantly, the rescue boat switched on its searchlight and turned.

Tired with his exertions, Wilberforce turned

too, and dived for the camp—blabble-abble-ebble-ibble-obble-obble-ubble-ubble-oomf.

'Did they find him?' asked Melody.

'They will,' said Wilberforce as the rescue boat's hull passed overhead, throbbing steadily —thrum-thrum-thrum-thrum.

'Good old Wilberforce,' said Melody.

'I'm tired,' said Wilberforce; 'you've no idea what it's like up there.'

'So am I,' said Melody, snuggling into the sand. 'I shall sleep the storm out.'

'Me too!' said Nelson, scuttling into his carpet-bag, and then one eye and a feeler returned. 'Until tomorrow!' he said.

6

A Day of Mixed Adventures

The storm had quite blown over the next morning, and a cheerful sun warmed a seascape dotted with islands. The wrecked yacht had already been towed clear, so it had evidently not been damaged too badly.

'Everybody ready?' called Wilberforce. 'Then man the capstan and weigh the anchor, my dibbly deckhands, and forward!'

'Forward which way?' asked Nelson.

'Well, forward forward, of course,' said Wilberforce, 'the way we're facing, nor'-by-nor'-west with just a trace of east by south in the general bearing,' he added, giving a jaunty nod with the admiral's cocked hat he was affecting for the day.

'But if we do that we shall run straight into all those islands,' said Melody.

'Then we must swim round them, my nautical niblet,' replied the whale laughing good-naturedly.

'But that will be *miles!*'

'Perhaps there's a channel through,' suggested Nelson.

'Now there's reason, there's ratiocination, there's *brains* for you,' cried Wilberforce admiringly. 'Let's see if we can find the short cut our nobby little navigator suggests.'

And off they set, with Nelson on the bridge and Melody in the cabin. There was just a suggestion of a swell, and as he rose and fell with it, Wilberforce sang:

> 'Hooray, and up she rises!
> Hooray, and up she rises!
> Hooray, and up she rises!
> Early in the morning.'

'If you sing when I'm here in the cabin,' said Melody, 'it tickles; the water goes all gurgly!'

They were cruising between two of the islands, and the cliffs on either side started to draw closer together, while the channel grew noticeably narrower.

'Just you wait, maties,' said Wilberforce. 'Any moment now it'll suddenly widen out into the open sea again.' And he swam—per-rump-ah, per-rump-ah, per-rump-ah—'I think,' he added—per-rump-ah, per-rump-ah—'At least it ought to.'—per-rump-ah—'Bother!' said Wilberforce.

'Bother!' echoed Nelson.

'Oh dear,' said Melody, 'now we shall have to go all the way back again.'

For the two islands had joined in a single steep cliff, which quite kept out the sun and completely blocked their way. Wilberforce hesitated a moment. Then he said:

'Perhaps we shan't have to go back; I can feel a current flowing.'

'Yes, look!' cried Nelson pointing downwards with one of his claws. And just below the surface of the sea was the mouth of a cave.

'Do you think it could be a tunnel?' cried Melody. 'Oh, how exciting! Can we go through it, Wilberforce?'

'I'm sure it is,' answered Wilberforce, 'I can feel the water moving. Come on; let's go down and see!'

And with his two small friends tightly gripping his right front fin, he flipped his great fluke-tail, and — blabble-abble-ebble-ibble-obble-ubble—down they dived.

It was quite a big tunnel lined almost to the roof with sea-thongs, and at the far end, a long, long way away, you could clearly see the other opening, a tiny round circle of light. Melody led the way in—pfut-pfut-pfut—and Nelson scuttled along the bottom, with Wilberforce a little way behind.

It was an exciting tunnel, very dark, but light

at each end, and it made Melody feel all 'Oo-oo-oo-er' in her tummy, but then you only had to look at the round sunlit hole at the far end and think of good old Wilberforce just behind for it to be all right. So she and Nelson played at making themselves feel all 'Oo-oo-oo-er' in their tummies by getting right in among the sea-thongs, and it was most truly and trembly exciting.

It took longer to reach the far end than they had expected, but gradually the distant round patch of sunlight grew larger, and then quite suddenly the tunnel widened out into a second cave. The sun shone in quite brightly, and across the cave's mouth hung what looked like a curtain of fine translucent threads. They glistened in the sun, and with a cry of, 'How pretty!' Melody darted — pitcherpoop — towards them.

'Stop!' shouted Wilberforce in the voice he only used for emergencies. Melody pulled up on her tail.

'What's the matter?' she asked.

'It's Medusa, a Portuguese man-of-war.' said Wilberforce. 'One touch of those poisonous tendrils would completely paralyse a small creature like you, my little minnikin. Look!'

Melody looked up at the surface and saw the underside of the jellyfish's bloated orange bladder filled with air and the loathsome pendant polyps, blue violet and carmine with their silvery sheen, and the long thread-like tentacles into whose terrible, stinging grip they had all but swum.

'It's horrid,' quavered Nelson. 'What are you going to do, Wilberforce?'

'Well, first of all, you two little 'uns get right back in the cave well clear of his stings. Then I shall go up and blow him away.'

'Blow him away?'

'Yes! The Portuguese man-of-war has a fin on top which he uses as a sail for moving about. So I shall go up and puff him off! Now right to the back of the cave!'

'But won't he hurt you?'

'I shall keep well out of his way,' and up he went—per-roosh—to the surface.

The two little creatures cowered right back in the cave, and Nelson slipped his claw into Melody's for reassurance. Supposing Wilberforce got hurt and didn't come back! They could see the whale's tum below the surface, and he swam in a circle at a fair distance. Then they realised he must be blowing into the jellyfish's sail because the horrid creature started to drift away, first slowly, and then faster and faster as if Wilberforce had blown it from a sheltered cove out into the open sea

where the breeze had taken over; and this is just what had happened.

Then Wilberforce's head reappeared below the surface, and down he came towards them— blabble - abble - ebble - ibble - obble - obble - ubble-ubble-oomf.

'Well, that's seen *him* off,' he said, and they moved forward once more.

'I *do* hope we don't have any more adventures like that,' said Nelson, still looking a little sideways to where Medusa had disappeared.

'But think of all the time we saved with your short cut,' said Melody and broke into a cheering chant for the little crab:

'Let praises resound
For Nelson, who found
A short cut is quicker than going around.'

Nelson went quite pink, and asked her to chant it again, and he was so delighted that he asked for it six times over, till Melody began thinking it was about time to change the words.

Just then they saw a strange bulky object in the distance. It was lying on the sea floor quite surrounded by a swarm of small fish. As they came up with it they realised that it was a sunken steamer, and at the same moment, out of one open porthole darted a crowd of sprats; they dashed in at the next porthole, and a second later, out at the next.

'They're playing Follow-my-leader,' cried Melody. Then almost before she had finished speaking, a large prawn shot out from behind a stanchion, tapped her on the shoulder with one of his whiskers and cried:

'You're on!'

'On what?'

'It's tig, stupid,' said the prawn—pitcher-poop—and darted away again.

'Oh, have we got time to stay and play?' asked Melody.

'Please, Wilberforce,' added Nelson.

'Of course,' said the whale; 'go and enjoy yourselves. I'll have a quiet browse around.'

And what games they had! Hide-and-seek in the cabins; tig on the poop; a real steering wheel in the wheelhouse, and levers and cogs in a real engine-room. There was a galley, where you could play cooks, and a state room where you could play houses, and there was King-of-the-castle on the very tip of the mast-head, and there were so many bits and pieces to do things with and to make things with, that, as Melody said breathlessly, there never was an adventure playground like it.

At last, completely tired out, they swam down the port companion-way, and there was Wilberforce on the sandy floor with a grand picnic tea for them: sea pie, seaweed sand-wiches, red and green, and a special plate of cuttlefish for himself—everything they liked best. And they were so hungry that they ate for years without talking at all—well *quite* five minutes! Well you *do,* don't you!

When they had finished, Wilberforce stretched and said:

'Do you know what I'd like to do now?'

'No,' said Melody, 'What?'

'I'd like to swim up to the top slowly and quietly, not going anywhere, but just to enjoy the evening.'

'Why that would be lovely,' said Melody and Nelson together.

So they swam up quite gently—per-roosh, per-roosh, per-roosh. As they broke surface, the sun had just set over the western horizon, leaving the blue-grey clouds reflecting crimson and gold flecks on their underside. To the east a pearl-grey sea met a pearl-grey sky in a haze which made it hard to find the horizon. A fine curved crescent of moon was already up, and a lighthouse had started its night's work, two flashes and a long pause—plup-plup . . . plup-plup . . . plup-plup . . . The night closed in, purple and soft. One huge star hung brilliantly below the moon. Suddenly a necklace of twinkling diamond points shone out along a distant promenade. And now the other stars by millions and billions and trillions were sparkling too. Silently, out to sea, the green starboard navigation light of a big invisible coaster moved steadily and safely across the black velvet of the scene.

The three friends lay silent and quite still.

'Ah-ah-ah!' sighed Wilberforce.

'It's lovely,' whispered Melody. 'I think it's the loveliest night of the loveliest holiday ever,' she added.

'Me too,' said Nelson.

'And it's all the nicer,' added Wilberforce, 'because there's still tomorrow.'

And all three of them sighed with contentment, 'M-m-m-m-m!'

7

The Powerboat Race

Wilberforce's blue-black bulk ploughed steadily through a cheerful sea whipped up by what sailors like to call 'a nice hand breeze'. Nelson was on the bridge and was passing the time by playing pirates. A piece of seaweed made a villainous patch over one eye, and a sliver of razor shell served for a cutlass. He was hobbling from side to side of Wilberforce's back on a wooden leg made from part of a lolly stick thrown overboard from a passing pleasure steamer.

'Belay there, ye scurvy scum!' he cried as fiercely as his little voice allowed. 'I'll slit your wizzend and make you walk the plank! Mutiny, is it?' and he brandished his little cutlass. 'It takes more than fifty of you bilge-rats to frighten Black Jack Nelson. I'll keel-haul the lot of you! I'll . . .'

At this point unfortunately, his wooden leg gave way, and he completely lost his balance. Wilberforce shook with laughter at his antics.

'It isn't fair to laugh,' complained Nelson; 'you wouldn't do it any better.'

'You make the most blood-curdling buccaneer I ever met, my freebooting little friend,' Wilberforce soothed him.

So Nelson picked himself up and was just about to 'hang the lot of them from the yard-arm,' when Melody, who had been on the lookout in the cabin, cut in:

'Ahoy! Broken water ahead!'

And sure enough a short way off the waves were boiling and seething. As they watched, a large black shape jumped six feet clear into the air and landed 'splosh' in the water again, and then another and another, until they could see the whole area was a mass of leaping, darting forms and frothing sea.

'It's a school of dolphins,' said Wilberforce. 'Let's go and watch them play.'

But there was no need to go to the dolphins, because the whole party was swimming fast towards them, and it was only seconds later that there was a loud 'splosh' a couple of feet from Wilberforce's nose, and immediately a cheeky, beaky face with a large smile and two bright eyes popped out of the water and said:

'I'm Cuddy; who are you?'

'I'm Wilberforce Whale,' replied Wilberforce

as a second figure went 'splosh' two feet on the other side of him.

'And this is my sister, Cathy!'

'And these are my two special friends, Melody and Nelson.'

'Then let's have a game,' concluded Cuddy, and he and Cathy did a simultaneous back-flip right across Wilberforce's nose to change sides.

'I like skipping and jumping,' said Cathy. 'Come on!'

And then the whole school arrived, chattering and chittering and bleeping, because, of course, dolphins have a special Morse language of their own. And the fun was fast and furious. They leapt across Wilberforce's back; they double turned under his chin; and sometimes Wilberforce would give a little flip with his fluke-tail just timed to a nicety so that it sent them another three feet into the air doing a somersault, and this was so popular with the laughing creatures, that they all queued up for a turn. Others used his back as a water-chute, and some very cheeky ones swam underneath him and tickled his tum which made him laugh, and in fact, he laughed so much that he lost his grip on the chain holding the kedge-anchor, and all their luggage began to slide away down to the bottom. So Nelson and Melody went down too to look after it, because although they enjoyed the play, it was a bit rough for them and made them feel quite giddy.

Wilberforce and his new friends played on and on; he humped the whole length of himself to make them a switch-back, and he nibbled their tails and pretended he was going to eat them, and he made himself into a great arch for them to swim through.

And then, as quickly as they had arrived, the whole school said a cheery 'good-bye' and 'thank you very much' and 'I hope we shall meet again', and swam off chittering and chattering as noisily as ever, and Wilberforce rejoined the others on the sea-bed.

'Ha-ha-ha,' he panted and laughed at the same time. 'Huh-huh-huh . . . That was quite a morning! . . . and now, I think . . . luncheon!'

Wilberforce was quite hungry after his exertions, and Melody and Nelson also seemed to have picked up an appetite with all the excitement, and everyone ate very heartily indeed. So when the whale proposed a little nap after the meal, everyone agreed quite willingly, and they all settled down among the green leaf-weed, head to current and one by one they dropped off.

They were awakened by a terrible racket—b-rr-rr-mm, b-rr-rr-mm, b-rr-rr-mm!

'That's an outboard engine,' said Wilberforce; and as the noise grew louder, he added, 'That's twin outboards, a hundred horsepower at least, I should think.' Then, as the din reached a crescendo, 'It's powerboats racing!'

A great flat-bottomed hull roared overhead: b-rr-rr-mm, b-rr-rr-mm, b-rr-rr-mm. They could see the two propellers boiling in the water, and then it leapt quite out of sight, as the broad step hit a wave and the whole hull was thrown clear up into the air. Melody and Wilberforce thought they were a bit noisy, but Nelson was dancing with excitement:

'B-r-m, b-r-m,' he cried, 'b-r-m, b-r-m! Outboard racers! B-r-m! Let's go up and see them! B-r-m, b-r-m, b-r-m!'

So they went up, and there the great monsters were, flashing by at forty or fifty miles an hour, their bows right out of the water, their engines roaring, and their drivers in crash helmets and overalls fighting to control them as they bucketed from wave to wave, often leaping high in the air, just like the porpoises. They were of awesome size and each engine raced— b-rr-rr-mm, b-rr-rr-rr-rr—as the boat shot out of water, then b-rr-rr-mm as it hit the sea again.

They were racing three and four abreast in a wide swathe of sea. Suddenly one appeared on a course that headed straight for them. In the general din nobody heard the newcomer, and he was already on them when Nelson let out a cry of fear. Wilberforce did not even give an order. He pitched his two little friends into the sea on the safe side of his huge body, and started to turn head on to narrow the obstruction he offered to the tearing mechanical monster. The turn was only half complete, when there was a shuddering jar.

The boat leapt six feet into the air, heeled slightly over, hit the wave again twenty paces on, bucketed, rocked, gathered itself together and roared off. The driver did not even look back, but a mechanic peered over the side to see if they had been damaged. Perhaps they thought they had only struck a piece of driftwood.

But poor Wilberforce lay quite still. On the side of his head was a deep cut, and his eyes were wide open but glazed.

'Wilberforce,' cried Melody, 'are you all right? Oh, Wilberforce!'

But the whale made no reply. And then his huge body began to sink, down, slowly down, still and silent, and it was the stillness of that sinking body that was so terrible.

'Oh, Wilberforce, Wilberforce,' Melody cried. 'Whatever can I do? He mustn't sink and lie on the bottom, or he'll drown; he must come up to the surface for air.'

And still poor Wilberforce drifted silently, limply, down and down at a slight angle, until first his tail and then the rest of his body lay heavy and inert among the green leaf-weed at the bottom.

Melody swam very close to her old friend. '*Please,* Wilberforce, speak,' she said, and tears were starting behind her eyes.

'Please!' said Nelson.

And just at that terrible moment there was a faint sound in the distance. Was it a 'chirrup'? . . . It came nearer, and now the chattering and bleeping were unmistakable . . . The dolphins were back!

'Stay with him!' Melody cried to Nelson almost as sharply as Wilberforce himself would have done in such an emergency. Then she swam faster than she had ever swum before in her life—pfut-pfut-pfut-pfut-pfut!

The first porpoise she met was Cuddy.

'Cuddy, Cuddy, help!' she cried. 'Wilberforce has had a terrible accident . . . Hit by a boat! . . . He's . . . on the sea-bed . . . He doesn't move or speak!'

'Where?' said Cuddy.

Melody pointed.

'This way, everybody,' called Cuddy, 'and *fast!*'

The whole school had gone almost before Melody could turn round, and by the time she arrived back at the scene of the accident, twelve stalwart porpoises, six on each side, had their beaks under Wilberforce's great body and were starting to lift him up with a lot of: 'To me, Albert! A little more your way, George! Firmly, right under his tail, Julian!' and at last: 'Take your time from me,' said Cuddy, and all twelve of them began to lift so gently and skilfully as you would not have thought possible had you only seen them playing earlier in the morning. Meanwhile, Cathy and her special friend, Caroline, had been gathering fronds of bladder-locks to make a big bandage, and they tied this over the cut, which in fact stopped bleeding almost at once.

At length the porpoises had Wilberforce back on the surface, and Cathy swam up with a sponge to soothe his forehead. All the other porpoises lay round quietly in a huge circle watching and waiting in case they could be of any help, and Melody and Nelson trod water by their friend's great head. Then Wilberforce gave a little snort, and a feeble jet of air and water rose limply from his blow-hole. He shuddered all over, and all the porpoises lying round broke into a cheer.

'Ah, he's coming round,' said Cuddy. 'Now

all he needs is a good night's rest, and I expect he'll be better in the morning.'

'Oh, thank you, Cuddy; thank you, Cathy,' said Melody. 'What should we have done without you? . . . Oh I *do* hope he's better in the morning,' she went on.

'Me too. Oh me very much too,' whispered Nelson. 'Better tomorrow!'

8

An Unexpected Landfall

Cuddy and Cathy stayed to watch over Wilberforce all that night, changing his bandage and helping him to the surface when he needed to breathe. About midnight, as they lay gently rocking in the waves with Melody using her feelers ever so lightly to stroke the great nose and soothe it, Wilberforce fell into a comfortable sleep.

Although she hadn't meant to, Melody must have dropped off too, for the next thing she was conscious of was a single word:

'Luncheon!'

Pitcherpoop!—She swirled round, and Nelson and the two porpoises arrived almost as quickly.

'Wilberforce, you're better!'

'Better, my cheeky little chickadee, my shorty little shrimp, better than what?' Then he added, 'Oo-ooh, my head!'

'Better than before you had your bump.'

'Bump? I don't remember any particular

bump. Mind you, that play with you porpoises was a bit rough,' and he laughed at Cuddy who was standing by . . . 'Oo-ooh, my head!'

'It wasn't us porpoises,' said Cuddy; 'it was your crash with the powerboat.'

'And it isn't luncheon time, it's brekker,' put in Nelson.

'Brekker time? Powerboat?' said Wilberforce obviously puzzled.

So they told him all about his accident, but still he couldn't remember a thing after playing with Cuddy and Cathy and the others in the morning.

At last, 'I don't mind whether it's luncheon or brekker,' he concluded. 'I'm hungry.'

'Well, that's a good sign,' said Cathy. 'If you like to come down, I'll get something ready for you.'

So they did that, and Cathy insisted on giving Wilberforce the full invalid treatment and really 'lushing him up', as she put it, and old Wilberforce enjoyed ever moment of it so much that he said he'd willingly take on a whole fleet of powerboats every day if the result was to be waited on 'fluke, fin and every whim' by Cathy. And Melody did a special chant for him:

'Though hit on the head like a nail,
His courage and grit never fail,
A hero is Wilberforce Whale!'

And he lay there grinning all over his huge friendly old face.

During breakfast, Wilberforce's memory seemed to be coming back, and by the end of the meal, he could recall everything except the actual crash itself.

'That's usual with this sort of thing,' said Cuddy. 'I don't expect you ever will remember it.'

'I don't know that I really want to,' grinned the whale. 'But since I *have* had this bump, I should like to get on with the journey as quickly as possible—get there today if we can—don't want to have a headache out in the middle of the ocean—better with your own people, you know!'

And though Cathy thought he really ought to rest for a couple of days there was a good deal of sense in what he said. So they loaded up the luggage on the kedge-anchor for the last time and floated up to the surface—blubble-ubble-obble-obble-ibble-ebble-abble-abble-sfisch! — and all the porpoises, headed by Cuddy and Cathy, lined up to escort them for the start of their journey with Nelson on the bridge and Melody in the cabin. A little while later, Cuddy and Cathy and all their school waved 'good-bye' and 'Good luck!' gave a huge leap out of the water in salute, and turned away. 'Good-bye!' the three friends waved back. Then they were alone again.

'I think it'll be quickest if we go "submarine",' said Wilberforce a moment later.

'What's that?' asked Nelson.

'Well, you both travel in the cabin and I shut my mouth. It'll be a bit dark and dull for you, but I can swim over the waves or down below, wherever the going is best, and I don't have to worry about your being swamped or washed away.'

The two little fish readily saw the point of this, and though it *was* a little dull being shut in, they didn't complain. So Wilberforce ploughed ahead very fast indeed.

All that day they could feel him surging along—per-rump-ah, per-rump-ah, per-rump-ah—while they played I *can't* spy with my little eye, using all the things they would have seen if it hadn't been so dark, and Blind man's buff, which was very convenient because they didn't need a blindfold. But this wasn't a great success, because it was rather easy to guess who you had caught. Then Melody told Nelson a story about a shrimp who was an orphan, but through her goodness of heart got adopted by a rich prawn and married a prince, and Nelson replied with a story of a crab who turned himself into a flying saucer and went to Mars.

It was a very long day, and it was quite late in the evening before Wilberforce at last slowed down, and opened his mouth for them to get out. They were on the sea-bed, and as they swam out over the silver sand floor, Wilberforce said:

'I've made my first landfall! I'm sure I recognise that jagged double-tooth rock covered with braided-hair weed.'

'Me too!' said Nelson.

'But you can't, my little minny midge, you haven't been to Scotland before,' said Wilberforce.

'Oh!' said Nelson.

Then they swam and scuttled on quietly for a bit—pfut-pfut, and per-rump-ah, per-rump-ah. 'And then there's that large flat rock with one corner crumbling away, yes, I know that.'

'Me too!' said Nelson again.

'But you've never been here before, my wee crabby granule,' laughed Wilberforce. Then they all swam round the corner of this rock, and Wilberforce added, 'and there's that neat little cave, I know that!'

'And *I* know that,' cried Melody.

'And me jolly well too,' said Nelson.

'That's my cave,' she went on. Pitcherpoop!

—she darted in, and—pitcherpoop!—she darted out again. 'Yes, it *is* my cave!'

'It was your bump with the powerboat, Wilberforce,' she said. 'It must have done something to your sense of direction.'

'My bump of locality! Huh-huh-huh,' laughed Wilberforce. 'And come to mention it,' he cried, his face lighting up, 'when I said I was all right at breakfast, I was still really a bit wuzzy, but just this last minute my headache's quite gone, and I'm my old self again. I can remember everything now, and I've spent all today swimming in a great big circle! Oh well!' he said, 'If I can swim submarine all the way back here today, I can swim you there again tomorrow; we shan't be so very late in getting to my Aunty Barnacle's.'

So that was all right.

'But it's *nice* being home,' said Melody thoughtfully.

'Yes, my little shrimpy morsel,' agreed Wilberforce, and he broke into one of his rumbling songs:

> 'Wherever I may roam,
> Be it ever so humble,
> There's no place like home.'

Just then, round the corner of the rock covered in red leaf-weed, there scuttled another crab, just like Nelson but even tinier, and his little claws clutched a square of orange sailcloth.

'Hallo, Hardy!' said Nelson.

'Hallo, pieface!' replied Hardy, sticking out his tongue.

'Younger brothers!' Nelson turned disgustedly to Melody. 'Pieface! Did you hear that? Cheeky little brat! And if I lay a finger on him, our mum'll tie me twice round the lighthouse!'

'You haven't given me your second best penknife as you promised,' accused Hardy.

'I will when you've done the job,' replied his elder brother, and then, turning to Wilberforce, 'He's made me give it to him for doing my holiday job for me at the Post Office while I was away. What have you got there, Hardy?'

'It's a telegram for Wilberforce. It came just half an hour after you left.'

'A telegram! My, my, my, that's important! Read it, please, Nelson,' said Wilberforce.

So Nelson unfolded the piece of orange sailcloth and set to work scuttling from side to side to read it.

'It begins,' he said, 'TELEGRAPHIC ADDRESS: WILBERWHALE, SEA-BED.' Then it goes on: 'IF YOU HAVEN'T STARTED STOP STOP REGRET HAVE CONTRACTED MERMEASLES VERY CATCHING SO BETTER YOU SHOULD NOT COME AND STOP STOP

VERY DISAPPOINTED STOP COME AGAIN WHEN I
AM WELL AND STAY STOP STOP AS LONG AS YOU
LIKE STOP—SENDER BARNACLE.'

'What's it mean?' asked Hardy.

'Well,' said Nelson, 'I think the telegraph
clerk has spelt out the punctuation as well as
the words. I'm afraid Aunty Barnacle can't
have us to stay stop!'

'Stop!' cried Wilberforce. 'If we have any
more of this stuttering stop stop stuff, my
telegraphic little crablet, I shall probably put a
full stop to one of my little midgy friend's
career exclamation mark! In words of one
syllable and with*out* punctuation, my Aunty
Barnacle is ill, and we can't go and stay with
her until she's better.'

'What's mermeasles?' asked Hardy.

'Very spickily and tickily, not to mention
bumperly and humperly with touches of
excru-u-uciating rash. Like a sea-urchin with
pimples and turned inside out, and it itches
horrid.'

'Oh,' said Hardy, 'I don't think I should
like that.'

'Well, it *is* nice being back home, and there's
always another day to visit Wilberforce's Aunty
Barnacle,' said Melody philosophically.

'Yes,' said Wilberforce, 'I'm really glad to be
back.'

'Me too,' said Nelson.

So they took all the baggage off the kedge-anchor, and Melody said:

'I don't care if we didn't actually get there, it was a lovely holiday trip. Thank you so much, Wilberforce! You'll be round to play as usual?'

'Of course,' said Wilberforce. 'It was fun, wasn't it! Now I must be off. Goodbye!' and —per-roosh, per-roosh!—with two swishes of his great fluke-tail he disappeared into the braided-hair weed.

'I must go and unpack,' said Melody, picking up her vanity case. 'Good-bye,' she said, and—per-shoo-oot!—she disappeared into her cave.

'Oh well,' said Hardy and Nelson together, 'us too! Good-bye!' and they scuttled off sideways round the rock covered with red leaf-weed.